I N THE LITTLE GUEST HOUSE on the Riviera where I was staying at the time, ten years before the war, a heated discussion had broken out at our table and unexpectedly threatened to degenerate into frenzied argument, even rancour and recrimination. Most people have little imagination. If something doesn't affect them directly, does not drive a sharp wedge straight into their minds, it hardly excites them at all, but if an incident, however slight, takes place before their eyes, close enough for the senses to perceive it, it instantly rouses them to extremes of passion. They compensate for the infrequency of their sympathy, as it were, by exhibiting disproportionate and excessive vehemence.

Such was the case that day among our thoroughly bourgeois company at table, where on the whole we just made equable small talk and cracked mild little jokes, usually parting as soon as the meal was over: the German husband and wife to go on excursions and take snapshots, the portly Dane to set out on tedious fishing expeditions, the distinguished English lady to return to her books, the Italian married couple to indulge in escapades to Monte Carlo, and I to lounge in a garden chair or get some work done. This time, however, our irate discussion left us all still very much at odds, and if someone suddenly rose it was not, as usual, to take civil leave of the rest of us, but in a mood of heated irascibility that, as I have said, was assuming positively frenzied form.

The incident obsessing our little party, admittedly, was odd enough. From outside, the guest house where the seven of us were staying might have been an isolated villa—with a wonderful view of the rock-strewn beach from its windows—but in fact it was only the cheaper annexe of the Grand Palace Hotel to which it was directly linked by the garden, so that we in the guest house were in constant touch with the hotel guests. And that same hotel had been the scene of an outright scandal the day before, when a young Frenchman had arrived by the midday train, at twenty-past twelve (I can't avoid giving the time so precisely because it was of importance to the incident itself, and indeed to the subject of our agitated conversation), and took a room with a view of the sea, opening straight on to the beach, which in itself indicated that he was in reasonably easy circumstances. Not only his discreet elegance but, most of all, his extraordinary and very appealing good looks made an attractive impression. A silky blond moustache surrounded sensuously warm lips in a slender, girlish face; soft, wavy brown hair curled over his pale forehead; every glance of his melting eyes was a caress—indeed everything about him was soft, endearing, charming, but without any artifice or affectation.

STEFAN ZWEIG

Twenty-Four Hours in the Life of a Woman

Translated from the German by Anthea Bell

PUSHKIN PRESS

Pushkin Press
71–75 Shelton Street
London WC2H 9JQ

Original texts © Williams Verlag AG Zurich
Translation © Anthea Bell 2006
This translation first published by Pushkin Press in 2006

This edition first published in 2016

0 0 1

ISBN 978 1 782272 15 1

Set in Monotype Baskerville by Tetragon, London

Printed and bound by CPI Group (UK) Ltd, Croydon CRO 4YY

www.pushkinpress.com

At a distance he might at first remind you slightly of those pink wax dummies to be seen adopting dandified poses in the window displays of large fashion stores, walking-stick in hand and representing the ideal of male beauty, but closer inspection dispelled any impression of foppishness, for—most unusually—his charm was natural and innate, and seemed an inseparable part of him. He greeted everyone individually in passing, in a manner as warm as it was modest, and it was a pleasure to see his unfailingly graceful demeanour unaffectedly brought into play on every occasion. When a lady was going to the cloakroom he made haste to fetch her coat, he had a friendly glance or joke for every child, he was both affable and discreet—in short, he seemed to be one of those happy souls who, secure in the knowledge that their bright faces and youthful attractions are pleasing to others, transmute that security anew into yet more charm. His presence worked wonders among the hotel guests, most of whom were elderly and sickly, and he irresistibly won everyone's liking with the victorious bearing of youth, that flush of ease and liveliness with which charm so delightfully endows some human beings. Only a couple of hours after his arrival he was playing tennis with the two daughters of the stout, thick-set manufacturer from Lyon—twelve-year-old Annette and thirteen-year-old Blanche—and their mother, the refined, delicate and reserved Madame Henriette, smiled slightly to see her inexperienced daughters unconsciously flirting with the young stranger. That evening he watched for an hour as we played chess, telling a few amusing anecdotes now and then in an unobtrusive style, strolled along the terrace again with Madame Henriette while her husband played dominoes with a business friend as usual; and late in the evening I saw him in suspiciously intimate conversation with the hotel secretary in the dim light of her office. Next morning he went fishing with my Danish chess partner, showing a remarkable knowledge of angling, and then held a long conversation about politics with the Lyon manufacturer in which he also proved himself an entertaining companion, for the stout Frenchman's hearty laughter could be heard above the sound of the breaking waves. After lunch he spent an hour alone with Madame Henriette in the garden again, drinking black coffee, played another game of tennis with her daughters and chatted in the lobby to the German couple. At six o'clock I met him at the railway station when I went to post a letter. He strode quickly towards me and said, as if apologetically, that he had been suddenly called away but would be back in two days' time. Sure enough, he was absent from the dining room that evening, but only in person, for he was the sole subject of conversation at every table, and all the guests praised his delightful, cheerful nature.

That night, I suppose at about eleven o'clock, I was sitting in my room finishing a book when I suddenly heard agitated shouts and cries from the garden coming in through my open window. Something was obviously going on over at the hotel. Feeling concerned rather than curious, I immediately hurried across—it was some fifty paces—and found the guests and staff milling around in great excitement. Madame Henriette, whose husband had been playing dominoes with his friend from Namur as usual, had not come back from her evening walk on the terrace by the beach, and it was feared that she had suffered an accident. The normally ponderous, slow-moving manufacturer kept charging down to the beach like a bull, and when he called: "Henriette! Henriette!" into the night, his voice breaking with fear, the sound conveyed something of the terror and the primeval nature of a gigantic animal wounded to death. The waiters and pageboys ran up and down the stairs in agitation, all the guests were woken and the police were called. The fat man, however, trampled and stumbled his way through all this, waistcoat unbuttoned, sobbing and shrieking as he pointlessly shouted the name "Henriette! Henriette!" into the darkness. By now the children were awake upstairs, and stood at the window in their night dresses, calling down for their mother. Their father hurried upstairs again to comfort them.

And then something so terrible happened that it almost defies retelling, for a violent strain on human nature, at moments of extremity, can often give such tragic expression to a man's bearing that no images or words can reproduce it with the same lightning force. Suddenly the big, heavy man came down the creaking stairs with a changed look on his face, very weary and yet grim. He had a letter in his hand. "Call them all back!" he told the hotel major-domo, in a barely audible voice. "Call everyone in again. There's no need. My wife has left me."

Mortally wounded as he was, the man showed composure, a tense, superhuman composure as he faced all the people standing around, looking at him curiously as they pressed close and then suddenly turned away again, each of them feeling alarmed, ashamed and confused. He had just enough strength left to make his way unsteadily past us, looking at no one, and switch off the light in the reading room. We heard the sound of his ponderous, massive body dropping heavily into an armchair, and then a wild, animal sobbing, the weeping of a man who has never wept before. That elemental pain had a kind of paralysing power over every one of us, even the least of those present. None of the waiters, none of the guests who had joined the throng out of curiosity, ventured either a smile or a word of condolence. Silently, one by one, as if put to shame by so shattering an emotional outburst, we crept back to our rooms, while that stricken specimen of mankind shook and sobbed alone with himself in the dark as the building slowly laid itself to rest, whispering, muttering, murmuring and sighing.

You will understand that such an event, striking like lightning before our very eyes and our perceptions, was likely to cause considerable turmoil in persons usually accustomed to an easygoing existence and carefree pastimes. But while this extraordinary incident was certainly the point of departure for the discussion that broke out so vehemently at our table, almost bringing us to blows, in essence the dispute was more fundamental, an angry conflict between two warring concepts of life. For it soon became known from the indiscretion of a chambermaid who had read the letter—in his helpless fury, the devastated husband had crumpled it up and dropped it on the floor somewhere—that Madame Henriette had not left alone but, by mutual agreement, with the young Frenchman (for whom most people's liking now swiftly began to evaporate). At first glance, of course, it might seem perfectly understandable for this minor Madame Bovary to exchange her stout, provincial husband for an elegant and handsome young fellow. But what aroused so much indignation in all present was the circumstance that neither the manufacturer nor his daughters, nor even Madame Henriette herself, had ever set eyes on this Lovelace before, and consequently their evening conversation for a couple of hours on the terrace, and the one-hour session in the garden over black coffee, seemed to have sufficed to make a woman about thirty-three years old and of blameless reputation abandon her husband and two children overnight, following a young dandy previously unknown to her without a second thought. This apparently evident fact was unanimously condemned at our table as perfidious deceit and a cunning manoeuvre on the part of the two lovers: of course Madame Henriette must have been conducting a clandestine affair with the young man long before, and he had come here, Pied Piper that he was, only to settle the final details of their flight, for—so our company deduced—it was out of the question for a decent woman who had known a man a mere couple of hours to run off just like that when he first whistled her up. It amused me to take a different view, and I energetically defended such an eventuality as possible, even probable in a woman who at heart had perhaps been ready to take some decisive action through all the years of a tedious, disappointing marriage. My unexpected opposition quickly made the discussion more general, and it became particularly agitated when both married couples, the Germans and the Italians alike, denied the existence of the *coup de foudre* with positively scornful indignation, condemning it as folly and tasteless romantic fantasy.

Well, it's of no importance here to go back in every detail over the stormy course of an argument conducted between soup and dessert: only professionals of the table d'hôte are witty, and points made in the heat of a chance dispute at table are usually banal, since the speakers resort to them clumsily and in haste. It is also difficult to explain how our discussion came to assume the form of insulting remarks so quickly; I think it grew so vehement in the first place because of the instinctive wish of both husbands to reassure themselves that their own wives were incapable of such shallow inconstancy. Unfortunately they could find no better way of expressing their feelings than to tell me that no one could speak as I did except a man who judged the feminine psyche by a bachelor's random conquests, which came only too cheap. This accusation rather annoyed me, and when the German lady added her mite by remarking instructively that there were real women on the one hand and 'natural-born tarts' on the other, and in her opinion Madame Henriette must have been one of the latter, I lost patience entirely and became aggressive myself. Such a denial of the obvious fact that at certain times in her life a woman is delivered up to mysterious powers beyond her own will and judgement, I said, merely concealed fear of our own instincts, of the demonic element in our nature, and many people seemed to take pleasure in feeling themselves stronger, purer and more moral than those who are 'easily led astray'. Personally, I added, I thought it more honourable for a woman to follow her instincts freely and passionately than to betray her husband in his own arms with her eyes closed, as so many did. Such, roughly, was the gist of my remarks, and the more the others attacked poor Madame Henriette in a conversation now rising to fever pitch, the more passionately I defended her (going far beyond what I actually felt in the case). My enthusiasm amounted to what in student circles might have been described as a challenge to the two married couples, and as a not very harmonious quartet they went for me with such indignant solidarity that the old Dane, who was sitting there with a jovial expression, much like the referee at a football match with stopwatch in hand, had to tap his knuckles on the table from time to time in admonishment. "Gentlemen, please!" But it never worked for long. One of the husbands had jumped up from the table three times already, red in the face, and could be calmed by his wife only with difficulty—in short, a dozen minutes more and our discussion would have ended in violence, had not Mrs C suddenly poured oil on the stormy waters of the conversation.

Mrs C, the white-haired, distinguished old English lady, presided over our table as unofficial arbiter. Sitting very upright in her place, turning to everyone with the same uniform friendliness, saying little and yet listening with the most gratifying interest, she was a pleasing sight from the purely physical viewpoint, and an air of wonderfully calm composure emanated from her aristocratically reserved nature. Up to a certain point she kept her distance from the rest of us, although she could also show special kindness with tactful delicacy: she spent most of her time in the garden reading books, and sometimes played the piano, but she was seldom to be seen in company or deep in conversation. You scarcely noticed her, yet she exerted a curious influence over us all, for no sooner did she now, for the first time, intervene in our discussion than we all felt, with embarrassment, that we had been too loud and intemperate.

Mrs C had made use of the awkward pause when the German gentleman jumped brusquely up and was then induced to sit quietly down again. Unexpectedly, she raised her clear, grey eyes, looked at me indecisively for a moment, and then, with almost objective clarity, took up the subject in her own way.

"So you think, if I understand you correctly, that Madame Henriette—that a woman can be cast unwittingly into a sudden adventure, can do things that she herself would have thought impossible an hour earlier, and for which she can hardly be held responsible?"

"I feel sure of it, ma'am."

"But then all moral judgements would be meaningless, and any kind of vicious excess could be justified. If you really think that a *crime passionnel*, as the French call it, is no crime at all, then what is the state judiciary for? It doesn't take a great deal of good will—and you yourself have a remarkable amount of that," she added, with a slight smile, "to see passion in every crime, and use that passion to excuse it."

The clear yet almost humorous tone of her words did me good, and instinctively adopting her objective stance I answered half in jest, half in earnest myself: "I'm sure that the state judiciary takes a more severe view of such things than I do; its duty is to protect morality and convention without regard for pity, so it is obliged to judge and make no excuses. But as a private person I don't see why I should voluntarily assume the role of public prosecutor. I'd prefer to appear for the defence. Personally, I'd rather understand others than condemn them."

Mrs C looked straight at me for a while with her clear grey eyes, and hesitated. I began to fear she had failed to understand what I said, and was preparing to repeat it in English. But with a curious gravity, as if conducting an examination, she continued with her questions.

"Don't you think it contemptible or shocking, though, for a woman to leave her husband and her children to follow some chance-met man, when she can't even know if he is worth her love? Can you really excuse such reckless, promiscuous conduct in a woman who is no longer in her first youth, and should have disciplined herself to preserve her self-respect, if only for the sake of her children?"

"I repeat, ma'am," I persisted, "that I decline to judge or condemn her in this case. To you, I can readily admit that I was exaggerating a little just now—poor Madame Henriette is certainly no heroine, not even an adventuress by nature, let alone a *grande amoureuse*. So far as I know her, she seems to me just an average, fallible woman. I do feel a little respect for her because she bravely followed the dictates of her own will, but even more pity, since tomorrow, if not today, she is sure to be deeply unhappy. She may have acted unwisely and certainly too hastily, but her conduct was not base or mean, and I still challenge anyone's right to despise the poor unfortunate woman."

"And what about you yourself; do you still feel exactly the same respect and esteem for her? Don't you see any difference between the woman you knew the day before yesterday as a respectable wife, and the woman who ran off with a perfect stranger a day later?"

"None at all. Not the slightest, not the least difference."

"*Is that so?*" She instinctively spoke those words in English; the whole conversation seemed to be occupying her mind to a remarkable degree. After a brief moment's thought, she raised her clear eyes to me again, with a question in them.

"And suppose you were to meet Madame Henriette tomorrow, let's say in Nice on the young man's arm, would you still greet her?"

"Of course."

"And speak to her?"

"Of course."

"If… if you were married, would you introduce such a woman to your wife as if nothing had happened?"

"Of course."

"*Would you really?*" she said, in English again, speaking in tones of incredulous astonishment.

"*Indeed I would,*" I answered, unconsciously falling into English too.

Mrs C was silent. She still seemed to be thinking hard, and suddenly, looking at me as if amazed at her own courage, she said: "I don't know if I would. Perhaps I might." And with the indefinable and peculiarly English ability to end a conversation firmly but without brusque discourtesy, she rose and offered me her hand in a friendly gesture. Her intervention had restored peace, and we were all privately grateful to her for ensuring that although we had been at daggers drawn a moment ago, we could speak to each other with tolerable civility again. The dangerously charged atmosphere was relieved by a few light remarks.

Although our discussion seemed to have been courteously resolved, its irate bitterness had none the less left a faint, lingering sense of estrangement between me and my opponents in argument. The German couple behaved with reserve, while over the next few days the two Italians enjoyed asking me ironically, at frequent intervals, whether I had heard anything of '*la cara signora Henrietta*'. Urbane as our manners might appear, something of the equable, friendly good fellowship of our table had been irrevocably destroyed.

The chilly sarcasm of my adversaries was made all the more obvious by the particular friendliness Mrs C had shown me since our discussion. Although she was usually very reserved, and hardly ever seemed to invite conversation with her table companions outside meal times, she now on several occasions found an opportunity to speak to me in the garden and—I might almost say—distinguish me by her attention, for her upper-class reserve made a private talk with her seem a special favour. To be honest, in fact, I must say she positively sought me out and took every opportunity of entering into conversation with me, in so marked a way that had she not been a white-haired elderly lady I might have entertained some strange, conceited ideas. But when we talked our conversation inevitably and without fail came back to the same point of departure, to Madame Henriette: it seemed to give her some mysterious pleasure to accuse the errant wife of weakness of character and irresponsibility. At the same time, however, she seemed to enjoy my steadfast defence of that refined and delicate woman, and my insistence that nothing could ever make me deny my sympathy for her. She constantly steered our conversation the same way, and in the end I hardly knew what to make of her strange, almost eccentric obsession with the subject.

This went on for a few days, maybe five or six, and she never said a word to suggest why this kind of conversation had assumed importance for her. But I could not help realising that it had when I happened to mention, during a walk, that my stay here would soon be over, and I thought of leaving the day after tomorrow. At this her usually serene face suddenly assumed a curiously intense expression, and something like the shadow of a cloud came into her clear grey eyes. "Oh, what a pity! There's still so much I'd have liked to discuss with you." And from then on a certain uneasy restlessness showed that while she spoke she was thinking of something else, something that occupied and distracted her mind a great deal. At last she herself seemed disturbed by this mental distraction, for in the middle of a silence that had suddenly fallen between us she unexpectedly offered me her hand.

"I see that I can't put what I really want to say to you clearly. I'd rather write it down." And walking faster than I was used to seeing her move, she went towards the house.

I did indeed find a letter in her energetic, frank handwriting in my room just before dinner that evening. I now greatly regret my carelessness with written documents in my youth, which means that I cannot reproduce her note word for word, and can give only the gist of her request: might she, she asked, tell me about an episode in her life? It lay so far back in the past, she wrote, that it was hardly a part of her present existence any more, and the fact that I was leaving the day after tomorrow made it easier for her to speak of something that had occupied and preyed on her mind for over twenty years. If I did not feel such a conversation was an importunity, she would like to ask me for an hour of my time.

The letter—I merely outline its contents here—fascinated me to an extraordinary degree: its English style alone lent it great clarity and resolution. Yet I did not find it easy to answer. I tore up three drafts before I replied:

I am honoured by your showing such confidence in me, and I promise you an honest response should you require one. Of course I cannot ask you to tell me more than your heart dictates. But whatever you tell, tell yourself and me the truth. Please believe me: I feel your confidence a special honour.

The note made its way to her room that evening, and I received the answer next morning:

You are quite right: half the truth is useless, only the whole truth is worth telling. I shall do my best to hide nothing from myself or from you. Please come to my room after dinner—at the age of sixty-seven, I need fear no misinterpretation, but I cannot speak freely in the garden, or with other people near by. Believe me, I did not find it easy to make my mind up to take this step.

During the day we met again at table and discussed indifferent matters in the conventional way. But when we encountered each other in the garden she avoided me in obvious confusion, and I felt it both painful and moving to see this white-haired old lady fleeing from me down an avenue lined with pine trees, as shy as a young girl.

At the appointed time that evening I knocked on her door, and it was immediately opened; the room was bathed in soft twilight, with only the little reading lamp on the table casting a circle of yellow light in the dusk. Mrs C came towards me without any self-consciousness, offered me an armchair and sat down opposite me. I sensed that she had prepared mentally for each of these movements, but then came a pause, obviously unplanned, a pause that grew longer and longer as she came to a difficult decision. I dared not inject any remark into this pause, for I sensed a strong will wrestling with great resistance here. Sometimes the faint notes of a waltz drifted up from the drawing room below, and I listened intently, as if to relieve the silence of some of its oppressive quality. She too seemed to feel the unnatural tension of the silence awkward, for she suddenly pulled herself together to take the plunge, and began.

"It's only the first few words that are so difficult. For the last two days I have been preparing to be perfectly clear and truthful; I

22

hope I shall succeed. Perhaps you don't yet understand why I am telling all this to you, a stranger, but not a day, scarcely an hour goes by when I do not think of this particular incident, and you can believe me, an old woman now, when I say it is intolerable to spend one's whole life staring at a single point in it, a single day. Everything I am about to tell you, you see, happened within the space of just twenty-four hours in my sixty-seven years of life, and I have often asked myself, I have wondered to the point of madness, why a moment's foolish action on a single occasion should matter. But we cannot shake off what we so vaguely call conscience, and when I heard you speak so objectively of Madame Henriette's case I thought that perhaps there might be an end to my senseless dwelling on the past, my constant self-accusation, if I could bring myself to speak freely to someone, anyone, about that single day in my life. If I were not an Anglican but a Catholic, the confessional would long ago have offered me an opportunity of release by putting what I have kept silent into words—but that comfort is denied us, and so I make this strange attempt to absolve myself by speaking to you today. I know all this sounds very odd, but you agreed unhesitatingly to my suggestion, and I am grateful.

As I said, I would like to tell you about just one day in my life—all the rest of it seems to me insignificant and would be tedious listening for anyone else. There was nothing in the least out of the ordinary in the course of it until my forty-second year. My parents were rich landlords in Scotland, we owned large factories and leased out land, and in the usual way of the gentry in my country we spent most of the year on our estates but went to London for the season. I met my future husband at a party when I was eighteen. He was a second son of the well-known R family, and had served with the army in India for ten years. We soon married, and led the carefree life of our social circle: three months of the year in London, three months on our estates, and the rest of the time in hotels in Italy, Spain and France. Not the slightest shadow ever clouded our marriage, and we had two sons who are now grown up. When I was forty my husband suddenly died. He had returned from his years in the tropics with a liver complaint, and I lost him within the space of two terrible weeks. My elder son was already in the army, my younger son at university—so I was left entirely alone overnight, and used as I was to affectionate companionship, that loneliness was a torment to me. I felt I could not stay a day longer in the desolate house where every object reminded me of the tragic loss of my beloved husband, and so I decided that while my sons were still unmarried, I would spend much of the next few years travelling.

In essence, I regarded my life from that moment on as entirely pointless and useless. The man with whom I had shared every hour and every thought for twenty-three years was dead, my children did not need me, I was afraid of casting a cloud over their youth with my sadness and melancholy—but I wished and desired nothing any more for myself. I went first to Paris, where I visited shops and museums out of sheer boredom, but the city and everything else were strange to me, and I avoided company because I could not bear the polite sympathy in other people's eyes when they saw that I was in mourning. How those months of aimless, apathetic wandering passed I can hardly say now; all I know is that I had a constant wish to die, but not the strength to hasten the end I longed for so ardently.

In my second year of mourning, that is to say my forty-second year, I had come to Monte Carlo at the end of March in my unacknowledged flight from time that had become worthless and was more than I could deal with. To be honest, I came there out of tedium, out of the painful emptiness of the heart that wells up like nausea, and at least tries to nourish itself on small external stimulations. The less I felt in myself, the more strongly I was drawn to those places where the whirligig of life spins most rapidly. If you are experiencing nothing yourself, the passionate restlessness of others stimulates the nervous system like music or drama.

That was why I quite often went to the casino. I was intrigued to see the tide of delight or dismay ebbing and flowing in other people's faces, while my own heart lay at such a low ebb. In addition my husband, although never frivolous, had enjoyed visiting such places now and then, and with a certain unintentional piety I remained faithful to his old habits. And there in the casino began those twenty-four hours that were more thrilling than any game, and disturbed my life for years.

I had dined at midday with the Duchess of M, a relation of my family, and after supper I didn't feel tired enough to go to bed yet. So I went to the gaming hall, strolled among the tables without playing myself, and watched the mingled company in my own special way. I repeat, in my own special way, the way my dead husband had once taught me when, tired of watching, I complained of the tedium of looking at the same faces all the time: the wizened old women who sat for hours before venturing a single jetton, the cunning professionals, the *demi-mondaines* of the card table, all that dubious chance-met company which, as you'll know, is considerably less picturesque and romantic than it is always painted in silly novels, where you might think it the *fleur d'élégance* and aristocracy of Europe. Yet the casino of twenty years ago, when real money, visible and tangible, was staked and crackling banknotes, gold Napoleons and pert little five-franc pieces rained down, was far more attractive than it is today, with a solid set of folk on Cook's Tours tediously frittering their characterless gaming chips away in the grand, fashionably renovated citadel of gambling. Even then, however, I found little to stimulate me in the similarity of so many indifferent faces, until one day my husband, whose private passion was for chiromancy—that's to say, divination by means of the hand—showed me an unusual method of observation which proved much more interesting, exciting and fascinating than standing casually around. In this method you never look at a face, only at the rectangle of the table, and on the table only at the hands of the players and the way they move. I don't know if you yourself ever happen to have looked at the green table, just that green square with the ball in the middle of it tumbling drunkenly from number to number, while fluttering scraps of paper, round silver and gold coins fall like seedcorn on the spaces of the board, to be raked briskly away by the croupier or shovelled over to the winner like harvest bounty. If you watch from that angle, only the hands change—all those pale, moving, waiting hands around the green table, all emerging from the ever-different caverns of the players' sleeves, each a beast of prey ready to leap, each varying in shape and colour, some bare, others laden with rings and clinking bracelets, some hairy like wild beasts, some damp and writhing like eels, but all of them tense, vibrating with a vast impatience. I could never help thinking of a racecourse where the excited horses are held back with difficulty on the starting line in case they gallop away too soon; they quiver and buck and rear in just the same way. You can tell everything from those hands, from the way they wait, they grab, they falter;

you can see an avaricious character in a claw-like hand and a spendthrift in a relaxed one, a calculating man in a steady hand and a desperate man in a trembling wrist; hundreds of characters betray themselves instantly in their way of handling money, crumpling or nervously creasing notes, or letting it lie as the ball goes round, their hands now weary and exhausted. Human beings give themselves away in play—a cliché, I know, but I would say their own hands give them away even more clearly in gambling. Almost all gamblers soon learn to control their faces—from the neck up, they wear the cold mask of impassivity; they force away the lines around their mouths and hide their agitation behind clenched teeth, they refuse to let their eyes show uneasiness, they smooth the twitching muscles of the face into an artificial indifference, obeying the dictates of polite conduct. But just because their whole attention is concentrated on controlling the face, the most visible part of the body, they forget their hands, they forget that some people are watching nothing but those hands, guessing from them what the lips curved in a smile, the intentionally indifferent glances wish to conceal. Meanwhile, however, their hands shamelessly reveal their innermost secrets. For a moment inevitably comes when all those carefully controlled, apparently relaxed fingers drop their elegant negligence. In the pregnant moment when the roulette ball drops into its shallow compartment and the winning number is called, in that second every one of those hundred or five hundred hands spontaneously makes a very personal, very individual movement of primitive instinct. And if an observer like me, particularly well-informed as I was because of my husband's hobby, is used to watching the hands perform in this arena, it is more exciting even than music or drama to see so many different temperaments suddenly erupt. I simply cannot tell you how many thousands of varieties of hands there are: wild beasts with hairy, crooked fingers raking in the money like spiders; nervous, trembling hands with pale nails that scarcely dare to touch it; hands noble and vulgar, hands brutal and shy, cunning hands, hands that seem to be stammering—but each of these pairs of hands is different, the expression of an individual life, with the exception of the four or five pairs of hands belonging to the croupiers. Those hands are entirely mechanical, and with their objective, businesslike, totally detached precision function like the clicking metal mechanism of a gas meter by comparison with the extreme liveliness of the gamblers' hands. But even those sober hands produce a surprising effect when contrasted with their racing, passionate fellows; you might say they were wearing a different uniform, like policemen in the middle of a surging, agitated riot. And then there is the personal incentive of getting to know the many different habits and passions of individual pairs of hands within a few days; by then I had always made acquaintances among them and divided them, as if they were human beings, into those I liked and those I did not. I found the greed and incivility of some so repulsive that I would always avert my gaze from them, as if from some impropriety. Every new pair of hands to appear on the table, however, was a fresh experience and a source of curiosity to me; I often quite forgot to look at the face which, surrounded by a collar high above them, was set impassively on top of an evening shirt or a glittering décolletage, a cold social mask.

When I entered the gaming hall that evening, passed two crowded tables, reached a third, and was taking out a few coins, I was surprised to hear a very strange sound directly opposite me in the wordless, tense pause that seems to echo with silence and always sets in as the ball, moving sluggishly, hesitates between two numbers. It was a cracking, clicking sound like the snapping of joints. I looked across the table in amazement. And then I saw—I was truly startled!—I saw two hands such as I had never seen before, left and right clutching each other like doggedly determined animals, bracing and extending together and against one another with such heightened tension that the fingers' joints cracked with a dry sound like a nut cracking open. They were hands of rare beauty, unusually long, unusually slender, yet taut and muscular—very white, the nails pale at their tips, gently curving and the colour of mother-of-pearl. I kept watching

them all evening, indeed I kept marvelling at those extraordinary, those positively unique hands—but what surprised
and alarmed me so much at first was the passion in them,
their crazily impassioned expressiveness, the convulsive way
they wrestled with and supported each other. I knew at once
that I was seeing a human being overflowing with emotion,
forcing his passion into his fingertips lest it tear him apart.
And then—just as the ball, with a dry click, fell into place in
the wheel and the croupier called out the number—at that
very moment the two hands suddenly fell apart like a pair
of animals struck by a single bullet. They dropped, both of
them, truly dead and not just exhausted; they dropped with
so graphic an expression of lethargy, disappointment, instant
extinction, as if all was finally over, that I can find no words
to describe it. For never before or since have I seen such
speaking hands, hands in which every muscle was eloquent
and passion broke almost tangibly from the pores of the
skin. They lay on the green table for a moment like jellyfish
cast up by the sea, flat and dead. Then one of them, the
right hand, began laboriously raising itself again, beginning
with the fingertips; it quivered, drew back, turned on itself,
swayed, circled, and suddenly reached nervously for a jetton,
rolling the token uncertainly like a little wheel between the
tips of thumb and middle finger. And suddenly it arched,
like a panther arching its back, and shot forwards, positively

spitting the hundred-franc jetton out on the middle of the black space. At once, as if at a signal, the inactive, slumbering left hand was seized by excitement too; it rose, slunk, crawled over to its companion hand, which was trembling now as if exhausted by throwing down the jetton, and both hands lay there together trembling, the joints of their fingers working away soundlessly on the table, tapping slightly together like teeth chattering in a fever—no, I had never seen hands of such expressive eloquence, or such spasmodic agitation and tension. Everything else in this vaulted room, the hum from the other halls around it, the calls of the croupiers crying their wares like market traders, the movement of people and of the ball itself which now, dropped from above, was leaping like a thing possessed around the circular cage that was smooth as parquet flooring—all this diversity of whirling, swirling impressions flitting across the nerves suddenly seemed to me dead and dull compared to those two trembling, breathing, gasping, waiting, freezing hands, that extraordinary pair of hands which somehow held me spellbound.

But finally I could no longer refrain; I had to see the human being, the face to which those magical hands belonged, and fearfully—yes, I do mean fearfully, for I was afraid of those hands!—my gaze slowly travelled up the gambler's sleeves and narrow shoulders. And once again I had a shock, for his face spoke the same fantastically extravagant language of extremes as the hands, shared the same terrible grimness of expression and delicate, almost feminine beauty. I had never seen such a face before, a face so transported and utterly beside itself, and I had plenty of opportunity to observe it at leisure as if it were a mask, an unseeing sculpture: those possessed eyes did not turn to right or left for so much as a second, their pupils were fixed and black beneath the widely opened lids, dead glass balls reflecting that other mahogany-coloured ball rolling and leaping about the roulette wheel in such foolish high spirits. Never, I repeat, had I seen so intense or so fascinating a face. It belonged to a young man of perhaps twenty-four, it was fine-drawn, delicate, rather long and very expressive. Like the hands, it did not seem entirely masculine, but resembled the face of a boy passionately absorbed in a game—although I noticed none of that until later, for now the face was entirely veiled by an expression of greed and of madness breaking out. The thin mouth, thirsting and open, partly revealed the teeth: you could see them ten paces away, grinding feverishly while the parted lips remained rigid. A light-blond lock of hair clung damply to his forehead, tumbling forwards like the hair of a man falling, and a tic fluttered constantly around his nostrils as if little waves were invisibly rippling beneath the skin. The bowed head was moving instinctively further and further forwards; you felt it was being swept away with the whirling of the little ball, and now, for the first time, I understood the convulsive pressure of the hands. Only by the intense strain of pressing them together did the body, falling from its central axis, contrive to keep its balance. I had never—I must repeat it yet again—I had never seen a face in which passion showed so openly, with such shamelessly naked animal feeling, and I stared at that face, as fascinated and spellbound by its obsession as was its own gaze by the leaping, twitching movement of the circling ball. From that moment on I noticed nothing else in the room, everything seemed to me dull, dim and blurred, dark by comparison with the flashing fire of that face, and disregarding everyone else present I spent perhaps an hour watching that one man and every movement he made: the bright light that sparkled in his eyes, the convulsive knot of his hands loosening as if blown apart by an explosion, the parting of the shaking fingers as the croupier pushed twenty gold coins towards their eager grasp. At that moment the face looked suddenly bright and very young, the lines in it smoothed out, the eyes began to gleam, the convulsively bowed body straightened lightly, easily—he suddenly sat there as relaxed as a horseman, borne up by the sense of triumph, fingers toying lovingly, idly with the round coins, clinking them together, making them dance and jingle playfully. Then he turned his head restlessly again, surveyed the green table as if with the flaring nostrils of a young hound seeking the right scent, and suddenly, with one quick movement, placed all the coins on one rectangular space. At once the watchfulness, the tension returned. Once more the little waves, rippling galvanically, spread out from his lips, once again his hands were clasped, the boyish face disappeared behind greedy expectation until the spasmodic tension exploded and fell apart in disappointment: the face that had just looked boyish turned faded, wan and old, light disappeared from the burnt-out eyes, and all this within the space of a second as the ball came to rest on the wrong number. He had lost; he stared at the ball for a few seconds almost like an idiot, as if he did not understand, but as the croupier began calling to whip up interest, his fingers took out a few coins again. But his certainty was gone; first he put the coins on one space, then, thinking better of it, on another, and when the ball had begun to roll his trembling hand, on a sudden impulse, quickly added two crumpled banknotes.

This alternation of up and down, loss and gain, continued without a break for about an hour, and during that hour I did not, even for a moment, take my fascinated gaze from that ever-changing face and all the passions ebbing and flowing over it. I kept my eyes fixed on those magical hands, their every muscle graphically reflecting the whole range of the man's feelings as they rose and fell like a fountain. I had never watched the face of an actor in the theatre as intently as I watched this one, seeing the constant, changing shades of emotion flitting over it like light and shade moving over a landscape. I had never immersed myself so wholeheartedly in a game as I did in the reflection of this stranger's excitement. If someone had been observing me at that moment he would surely have taken my steely gaze for a state of hypnosis, and indeed my benumbed perception was something like that—I simply could not look away from the play of those features, and everything else in the room, the lights, the laughter, the company and its glances, merely drifted vaguely around me, a yellow mist with that face in the middle of it, a flame among flames. I heard nothing, I felt nothing, I did not notice people coming forwards beside me, other hands suddenly reaching out like feelers, putting down money or picking it up; I did not see the ball or hear the croupier's voice, yet I saw it all as if I were dreaming, exaggerated as in a concave mirror by the excitement and extravagance of those moving hands. For I did not have to look at the roulette wheel to know whether the ball had come to rest on red or black, whether it was still rolling or beginning to falter. Every stage of the game, loss and gain, hope and disappointment, was fierily reflected in the nerves and movements of that passionate face.

But then came a terrible moment—something that I had been vaguely fearing all this time, something that had weighed like a gathering thunderstorm on my tense nerves, and now suddenly ripped through them. Yet again the ball had fallen back into the shallow depression with that dry little click, yet again came the tense moment when two hundred lips held their breath until the croupier's voice announced the winning number—this time it was zero—while he zealously raked in the clinking coins and crackling notes from all sides. At that moment those two convulsively clasped hands made a particularly terrifying movement, leaping up as if to catch something that wasn't there and then dropping to the table again exhausted, with no strength in them, only the force of gravity flooding back. Then, however, they suddenly came to life yet again, feverishly retreating from the table to the man's own body, clambering up his torso like wild cats, up and down, left and right, nervously trying all his pockets to see if some forgotten coin might not have slipped into one of them. But they always came back empty, and the pointless, useless search began again ever more frantically, while the roulette wheel went on circling and others continued playing, while coins clinked, chairs were shifted on the floor, and all the small sounds, put together a hundredfold, filled the room with a humming note. I trembled, shaking with horror; I felt it all as clearly as if my own fingers were rummaging desperately for a coin in the pockets and folds of my creased garments. And suddenly, with a single abrupt movement, the man rose to his feet opposite me, like a man standing up when he suddenly feels unwell and must rise if he is not to suffocate. His chair crashed to the floor behind him. Without even noticing, without paying any attention to his surprised and abashed neighbours as they avoided his swaying figure, he stumbled away from the table.

The sight petrified me. For I knew at once where the man was going: to his death. A man getting to his feet like that was not on his way back to an inn, a wine bar, a wife, a railway carriage, to any form of life at all, he was plunging straight into the abyss. Even the most hardened spectator in that hellish gaming hall could surely have seen that the man had nothing to fall back on, not at home or in a bank or with a family, but had been sitting here with the last of his money, staking his life, and was now staggering away somewhere else, anywhere, but undoubtedly out of that life. I had feared all along, I had sensed from the first moment, as if by magic, that more than loss or gain was staked on the game, yet now it struck me like a bolt of dark lightning to see the life suddenly go out of his eyes and death cast its pale shadow over his still living face. Instinctively—affected as I was by his own graphic gestures—I clutched at myself while the man tore himself away from his place and staggered out, for his own uncertain gait was now transferred to my own body just as his tension had entered my veins and nerves. Then I was positively wrenched away, I had to follow him; my feet moved without my own volition. It was entirely unconscious, I did not do it of my own accord, it was something happening to me when, taking no notice of anyone, feeling nothing myself, I went out into the corridor leading to the doors.

He was standing at the cloakroom counter, and the attendant had brought him his coat. But his arms would no longer obey him, so the helpful attendant laboriously eased them into the sleeves, as if he were paralysed. I saw him automatically put his hand in his waistcoat pocket to give the man a tip, but his fingers emerged empty. Then he suddenly seemed to remember everything, awkwardly stammered something to the cloakroom attendant, and as before moved forwards abruptly and then stumbled like a drunk down the casino steps, where the attendant stood briefly watching him go, with a smile that was at first contemptuous and then understanding.

His bearing shook me so much that I felt ashamed to have seen it. Involuntarily I turned aside, embarrassed to have watched a stranger's despair as if I were in a theatre—but then that vague fear suddenly took me out of myself once again. Quickly, I retrieved my coat, and thinking nothing very definite, purely mechanically and compulsively I hurried out into the dark after the stranger."

Mrs C interrupted her story for a moment. She had been sitting calmly opposite me, speaking almost without a break with her characteristic tranquil objectivity, as only someone who had prepared and carefully organised the events of her tale in advance could speak. Now, for the first time, she stopped, hesitated, and then suddenly broke off and turned directly to me.

"I promised you and myself," she began, rather unevenly, "to tell you all the facts with perfect honesty. Now I must ask you to believe in my honesty, and not assume that my conduct had any ulterior motives. I might not be ashamed of them today, but in this case such suspicions would be entirely unfounded. And I must emphasise that, when I hurried after that ruined gambler in the street, I had certainly not fallen in love with him—I did not think of him as a man at all, and indeed I was over forty myself at the time and had never looked at another man since my husband's death. All that part of my life was finally over; I tell you this explicitly, and I must, or you would not understand the full horror of what happened later. On the other hand, it's true that I would find it difficult to give a clear name to the feeling that drew me so compulsively after the unfortunate man; there was curiosity in it, but above all a dreadful fear, or rather a fear of something dreadful, something I had felt invisibly enveloping the young man like a miasma from the first moment. But such feelings can't be dissected and taken apart, if only because they come over one too compulsively, too fast, too spontaneously—very likely mine expressed nothing but the instinct to help with which one snatches back a child about to run into the road in front of a motor car. How else can we explain why non-swimmers will jump off a bridge to help a drowning man? They are simply impelled to do it as if by magic, some other will pushes them off the bridge before they have time to consider the pointless bravery of their conduct properly; and in just the same way, without thinking, without conscious reflection, I hurried after the unfortunate young man out of the gaming room, to the casino doors, out of the doors and on to the terrace.

And I am sure that neither you nor any other feeling human being with his eyes open could have withstood that fearful curiosity, for a more disturbing sight can hardly be imagined than the way the gambler, who must have been twenty-four at the most but moved as laboriously as an old man and was swaying like a drunk, dragged himself shakily and disjoint-edly down the steps to the terrace beside the road. Once there, his body dropped on to a bench, limp as a sack. Again I shuddered as I sensed, from that movement, that the man had reached the end of his tether. Only a dead man or one with nothing left to keep him alive drops like that. His head, fallen to one side, leant back over the bench, his arms hung limp and shapeless to the ground, and in the dim illumina-tion of the faintly flickering street lights any passer-by would have thought he had been shot. And it was like that—I can't explain why the vision suddenly came into my mind, but all of a sudden it was there, real enough to touch, terrifying and terrible—it was like that, as a man who had been shot, that I saw him before me at that moment, and I knew for certain that he had a revolver in his pocket, and tomorrow he would be found lying lifeless and covered with blood on this or some other bench. For he had dropped like a stone falling into a deep chasm, never to stop until it reaches the bottom: I never saw such a physical expression of exhaustion and despair.

So now, consider my situation: I was standing twenty or thirty paces from the bench and the motionless, broken man on it, with no idea what to do, on the one hand wishing to help, on the other restrained by my innate and inbred reluctance to speak to a strange man in the street. The gaslights flickered dimly in the overcast sky, few figures hurried past, for it was nearly midnight and I was almost entirely alone in the park with this suicidal figure. Five or ten times I had already pulled myself together and approached him, but shame or perhaps that deeper premonitory instinct, the idea that falling men are likely to pull those who come to their aid down with them, made me withdraw—and in the midst of this indecision I was clearly aware of the pointless, ridiculous aspect of the situation. Nonetheless, I could neither speak nor turn away, I could not do anything but I could not leave him. And I hope you will believe me when I say that for perhaps an hour, an endless hour, I walked indecisively up and down that terrace, while time was divided up by thousands of little sounds from the breaking waves of the invisible sea—so shaken and transfixed was I by the idea of the annihilation of a human being.

Yet I could not summon up the courage to say a word or make a move, and I would have waited like that half the night, or perhaps in the end my wiser self-interest would have prevailed on me to go home, and indeed I think I had already made up my mind to leave that helpless bundle of misery lying there—when a superior force put an end to my indecision. It began to rain. All evening the wind had been piling up heavy spring clouds full of moisture above the sea, lungs and heart felt the pressure of the lowering sky, and now drops suddenly began to splash down. Soon a heavy rain was falling in wet torrents blown about by the wind. I instinctively sheltered under the projecting roof of a kiosk, but although I put up my umbrella gusts of wind kept blowing the rain on my dress. I felt the cold mist thrown up by the falling raindrops spray my face and hands.

But—and it was such a terrible sight that even now, two decades later, the memory still constricts my throat—but in the middle of this cloudburst the unfortunate man stayed perfectly still on his bench, never moving. Water was gurgling and dripping from all the eaves; you could hear the rumble of carriages from the city; people with their coat collars turned up hurried past to right and to left; all living creatures ducked in alarm, fled, ran, sought shelter; man and beast felt universal fear of the torrential element—but that black heap of humanity on the bench did not stir or move. I told you before that he had the magical gift of graphically expressing everything he felt in movement and gesture. But nothing, nothing on earth could convey despair, total self-surrender, death in the midst of life to such shattering effect as his immobility, the way he sat there in the falling rain, not moving, feeling nothing, too tired to rise and walk the few steps to the shelter of the projecting roof, utterly indifferent to his own existence. No sculptor, no poet, not Michelangelo or Dante has ever brought that sense of ultimate despair, of ultimate human misery so feelingly to my mind as the sight of that living figure letting the watery element drench him, too weary and uncaring to make a single move to protect himself.

That made me act; I couldn't help it. Pulling myself together, I ran the gauntlet of the lashing rain and shook the dripping bundle of humanity to make him get up from the bench. 'Come along!' I seized his arm. Something stared up at me, with difficulty. Something in him seemed to be slowly preparing to move, but he did not understand. 'Come along!' Once again, almost angry now, I tugged at his wet sleeve. Then he slowly stood up, devoid of will and swaying. 'What do you want?' he asked, and I could not reply, for I myself had no idea where to take him—just away from the cold downpour where he had been sitting so senselessly, suicidally, in the grip of deep despair. I did not let go of his arm but dragged the man on, since he had no will of his own, to the sales kiosk where the narrow, projecting roof at least partly sheltered him from the raging attack of the stormy rain as the wind tossed it wildly back and forth. That was all I wanted, I had nothing else in mind, just to get him somewhere dry, under a roof. As yet I had thought no further.

So we stood side by side on that narrow strip of dry ground, the wall of the kiosk behind us and above us only the roof, which was not large enough, for the insatiable rain insidiously came in under it as sudden gusts of wind flung wet, chilly showers over our clothes and into our faces. The situation became intolerable. I could hardly stand there any longer beside this dripping wet stranger. On the other hand, having dragged him over here I couldn't just leave him and walk away without a word. Something had to be done, and gradually I forced myself to think clearly. It would be best, I thought, to send him home in a cab and then go home myself; he would be able to look after himself tomorrow. So as he stood beside me gazing fixedly out at the turbulent night I asked, 'Where do you live?'

'I'm not staying anywhere… I only arrived from Nice this morning… we can't go to my place.'

I did not immediately understand this last remark. Only later did I realise that the man took me for... for a *demi-mondaine*, one of the many women who haunt the casino by night, hoping to extract a little money from lucky gamblers or drunks. After all, what else was he to think, for only now that I tell you about it do I feel all the improbability, indeed the fantastic nature of my situation—what else was he to think of me? The way I had pulled him off the bench and dragged him away as if it were perfectly natural was certainly not the conduct of a lady. But this idea did not occur to me at once. Only later, only too late did his terrible misapprehension dawn upon me, or I would never have said what I did next, in words that were bound to reinforce his impression. 'Then we'll just take a room in a hotel. You can't stay here. You must get under cover somewhere.'

Now I understood his painful misunderstanding, for he did not turn towards me but merely rejected the idea with a certain contempt in his voice: 'I don't need a room; I don't need anything now. Don't bother, you won't get anything out of me. You've picked the wrong man. I have no money.'

This too was said in a dreadful tone, with shattering indifference, and the way he stood there dripping wet and leaning against the wall, slack and exhausted to the bone, shook me so much that I had no time to waste on taking petty offence. I merely sensed, as I had from the first moment when I saw him stagger from the gaming hall, as I had felt all through this improbable hour, that here was a human being, a young, living, breathing human being on the very brink of death, and I must save him. I came closer.

'Never mind money, come along! You can't stay here. I'll get you under cover. Don't worry about anything, just come with me.'

He turned his head and I felt, while the rain drummed round us with a hollow sound and the eaves cast water down to splash at our feet, that for the first time he was trying to make out my face in the dark. His body seemed to be slowly shaking off its lethargy too.

'As you like,' he said, giving in. 'It's all one to me… after all, why not? Let's go.' I put up my umbrella, he moved to my side and took my arm. I felt this sudden intimacy uncomfortable; indeed, it horrified me. I was alarmed to the depths of my heart. But I did not feel bold enough to ask him to refrain, for if I rejected him now he would fall into the bottomless abyss, and everything I had tried to do so far would be in vain. We walked the few steps back to the casino, and only now did it strike me that I had no idea what to do with him. I had better take him to a hotel, I thought quickly, and give him money to spend the night there and go home in the morning. I was not thinking beyond that. And as the carriages were now rapidly drawing up outside the casino I hailed a cab and we got in.

When the driver asked where to, I couldn't think what to say at first. But realising that the drenched, dripping man beside me would not be welcome in any of the best hotels—on the other hand, genuinely inexperienced as I was, with nothing else in mind—I just told the cabby, 'Some simple hotel, anywhere!'

The driver, indifferent, and wet with rain himself, drove his horses on. The stranger beside me said not a word, the wheels rattled, the rain splashed heavily against the windows, and I felt as if I were travelling with a corpse in that dark, lightless rectangular space, in a vehicle like a coffin. I tried to think of something to say to relieve the strange, silent horror of our presence there together, but I could think of nothing. After a few minutes the cab stopped. I got out first and paid the driver, who shut the door after us as if drunk with sleep. We were at the door of a small hotel that was unknown to me, with a glass porch above us providing a tiny area of shelter from the rain, which was still lashing the impenetrable night around us with ghastly monotony.

The stranger, giving way to his inertia, had instinctively leant against the wall, and water was dripping from his wet hat and crumpled garments. He stood there like a drunk who has been fished out of the river, still dazed, and a channel of water trickling down from him formed around the small patch of ground where he stood. But he made not the slightest effort to shake himself or take off the hat from which raindrops kept running over his forehead and face. He stood there entirely apathetically, and I cannot tell you how his broken demeanour moved me.

But something had to be done. I put my hand into my bag. 'Here are a hundred francs,' I said. 'Take a room and go back to Nice tomorrow.'

He looked up in astonishment.

'I was watching you in the gaming hall,' I continued urgently, noticing his hesitation. 'I know you've lost everything, and I fear you're well on the way to doing something stupid. There's no shame in accepting help—here, take it!'

But he pushed away my hand with an energy I wouldn't have expected in him. 'You are very good,' he said, 'but don't waste your money. There's no help for me now. Whether I sleep tonight or not makes not the slightest difference. It will all be over tomorrow anyway. There's no help for me.'

'No, you must take it,' I urged. 'You'll see things differently tomorrow. Go upstairs and sleep on it. Everything will look different in daylight.'

But when I tried to press the money on him again he pushed my hand away almost violently. 'Don't,' he repeated dully. 'There's no point in it. Better to do it out of doors than leave blood all over their room here. A hundred or even a thousand francs won't help me. I'd just go to the gaming hall again tomorrow with the last few francs, and

I wouldn't stop until they were all gone. Why begin again? I've had enough.'

You have no idea how that dull tone of voice went to my heart, but think of it: a couple of inches from you stands a young, bright, living, breathing human being, and you know that if you don't do your utmost, then in a few hours time this thinking, speaking, breathing specimen of youth will be a corpse. And now I felt a desire like rage, like fury, to overcome his senseless resistance. I grasped his arm. 'That's enough stupid talk. You go up these steps now and take a room, and I'll come in the morning and take you to the station. You must get away from here, you must go home tomorrow, and I won't rest until I've seen you sitting in the train with a ticket. You can't throw your life away so young just because you've lost a couple of hundred francs, or a couple of thousand. That's cowardice, silly hysteria concocted from anger and bitterness. You'll see that I'm right tomorrow!'

'Tomorrow!' he repeated in a curiously gloomy, ironic tone. 'Tomorrow! If you knew where I'd be tomorrow! I wish I knew myself—I'm mildly curious to find out. No, go home, my dear, don't bother about me and don't waste your money.'

But I wasn't giving up now. It had become like a mania obsessing me. I took his hand by force and pressed the banknote into it. 'You will take this money and go in at once!' And so saying I stepped firmly up to the door and rang the bell.

'There, now I've rung, and the porter will be here in a minute. Go in and lie down. I'll be outside here at nine tomorrow to take you straight to the station. Don't worry about anything, I'll see to what's necessary to get you home. But now go to bed, have a good sleep, and don't think of anything else!'

At that moment the key turned inside the door and the porter opened it.

'Come on, then!' said my companion suddenly, in a harsh, firm embittered voice, and I felt his fingers span my wrist in an iron grip. I was alarmed… so greatly alarmed, so paralysed, struck as if by lightning, that all my composure vanished. I wanted to resist, tear myself away, but my will seemed numbed, and I… well, you will understand… I was ashamed to struggle with a stranger in front of the porter, who stood there waiting impatiently. And so, suddenly, I was inside the hotel. I wanted to speak, say something, but my throat would not obey me… and his hand lay heavy and commanding on my arm. I vaguely felt it draw me as if unawares up a flight of steps—a key clicked in a lock. And suddenly I was alone with this stranger in a strange room, in some hotel whose name I do not know to this day."

Mrs C stopped again, and suddenly rose to her feet. It seemed that her voice would not obey her any more. She went over

51

to the window and looked out in silence for some minutes, or perhaps she was just resting her forehead on the cold pane; I did not have the courage to look closely, for I found it painful to see the old lady so agitated. So I sat quite still, asking no questions, making no sound, and waited until she came back, stepping firmly, and sat down opposite me.

"Well—now the most difficult part is told. And I hope you will believe me when I assure you yet again, when I swear by all that is sacred to me, by my honour and my children, that up to that moment no idea of any… any relationship with the stranger had entered my mind, that I really had been suddenly plunged into this situation against my own will, indeed entirely unawares, as if I had fallen through a trapdoor from the level path of my existence. I have promised to be honest with you and with myself, so I repeat again that I embarked on this tragic venture merely through a rather overwrought desire to help, not through any other, any personal feeling, quite without any wishes or forebodings.

You must spare me the tale of what happened in that room that night; I myself have forgotten not a moment of it, and I never will. I spent it wrestling with another human being for his life, and I repeat, it was a battle of life and death. I felt only too clearly, with every fibre of my being, that this stranger, already half-lost, was clutching at his last chance with all the avid passion of a man threatened by death. He clung to me like one who already feels the abyss yawning beneath him. For my part, I summoned everything in me to save him by all the means at my command. A human being may know such an hour perhaps only once in his life, and out of millions, again, perhaps only one will know it—but for that terrible chance I myself would never have guessed how ardently, desperately, with what boundless greed a man given up for lost will still suck at every red drop of life. Kept safe for twenty years from all the demonic forces of existence, I would never have understood how magnificently, how fantastically Nature can merge hot and cold, life and death, delight and despair together in a few brief moments. And that night was so full of conflict and of talk, of passion and anger and hatred, with tears of entreaty and intoxication, that it seemed to me to last a thousand years, and we two human beings who fell entwined into its chasm, one of us in frenzy, the other unsuspecting, emerged from that mortal tumult changed, completely transformed, senses and emotions transmuted.

But I don't want to talk about that. I cannot and will not describe it. However, I must just tell you of the extraordinary moment when I woke in the morning from a leaden sleep, from nocturnal depths such as I had never known before. It took me a long time to open my eyes, and the first thing I saw was a strange ceiling over me, and then, looking further an entirely strange, unknown, ugly room. I had no idea how I came to be there. At first I told myself I must still be dreaming, an unusually lucid, transparent dream into which I had passed from my dull, confused slumber—but the sparkling bright sunshine outside the windows was unmistakably genuine, the light of morning, and the sounds of the street echoed from below, the rattle of carriages, the ringing of tram bells, the noise of people—so now I knew that I was awake and not dreaming. I instinctively sat up to get my bearings, and then—as my glance moved sideways—then I saw, and I can never describe my alarm to you, I saw a stranger sleeping in the broad bed beside me… a strange, perfectly strange, half-naked, unknown man… oh, I know there's no real way to describe the awful realisation; it struck me with such terrible force that I sank back powerless. But not in a kindly faint, not falling unconscious, far from it: with lightning speed, everything became as clear to me as it was inexplicable, and all I wanted was to die of revulsion and shame at suddenly finding myself in an unfamiliar bed in a decidedly shady hotel, with a complete stranger beside me. I still remember how my heart missed a beat, how I held my breath as if that would extinguish my life and above all my consciousness, which grasped everything yet understood none of it.

I shall never know how long I lay like that, all my limbs icy cold: the dead must lie rigid in their coffins in much the same way. All I know is that I had closed my eyes and was praying to God, to some heavenly power, that this might not be true, might not be real. But my sharpened senses would not let me deceive myself, I could hear people talking in the next room, water running, footsteps shuffling along the corridor outside, and each of these signs mercilessly proved that my senses were terribly alert.

How long this dreadful condition lasted I cannot say: such moments are outside the measured time of ordinary life. But suddenly another fear came over me, swift and terrible: the stranger whose name I did not know might wake up and speak to me. And I knew at once there was only one thing to do: I must get dressed and make my escape before he woke. I must not let him set eyes on me again, I must not speak to him again. I must save myself before it was too late, go away, away, away, back to some kind of life of my own, to my hotel, I must leave this pernicious place, leave this country, never meet him again, never look him in the eye, have no witnesses, no accusers, no one who knew. The idea dispelled my faintness: very cautiously, with the furtive movements of a thief, I inched out of bed (for I was desperate to make no noise) and groped my way over to my clothes. I dressed very carefully, trembling all the time lest he might wake up, and then I had finished, I had done it. Only my hat lay at the foot of the bed on the far side of the room, and then, as I tiptoed over to pick it up—I couldn't help it, at that moment I had to cast another glance at the face of the stranger who had fallen into my life like a stone dropping off a window sill. I meant it to be just one glance, but it was curious—the strange young man who lay sleeping there really was a stranger to me. At first I did not recognise his face from yesterday. The impassioned, tense, desperately distressed features of the mortally agitated man might have been entirely extinguished—this man's face was not the same, but was an utterly childlike, utterly boyish face that positively radiated purity and cheerfulness. The lips, so grim yesterday as he clenched his teeth on them, were dreaming, had fallen softly apart, half-curving in a smile; the fair hair curled gently over the smooth forehead, the breath passed from his chest over his body at repose like the mild rippling of waves.

Perhaps you may remember that I told you earlier I had never before seen greed and passion expressed with such outrageous extravagance by any human being as by that stranger at the gaming table. And I tell you now that I had never, even in children whose baby slumbers sometimes cast an angelic aura of cheerfulness around them, seen such an expression of brightness, of truly blissful sleep. The uniquely graphic nature of that face showed all its feelings, at present the paradisaical easing of all internal heaviness, a sense of freedom and salvation. At this surprising sight all my own fear and horror fell from me like a heavy black cloak—I was no longer ashamed, no, I was almost glad. The terrible and incomprehensible thing that had happened suddenly made sense to me; I was happy, I was proud to think that but for my dedicated efforts the beautiful, delicate young man lying here carefree and quiet as a flower would have been found somewhere on a rocky slope, his body shattered and bloody, his face ruined, lifeless, with staring eyes. I had saved him; he was safe. And now I looked—I cannot put it any other way—I looked with maternal feeling at the man I had reborn into life more painfully than I bore my own children. In the middle of that shabby, threadbare room in a distasteful, grubby house of assignation, I was overcome by the kind of emotion—ridiculous as you may find it put into words—the kind of emotion one might have in church, a rapturous sense of wonder and sanctification. From the most dreadful moment of a whole life there now grew a second life, amazing and overwhelming, coming in sisterly fashion to meet me.

Had I made too much noise moving about? Had I involuntarily exclaimed out loud? I don't know, but suddenly the sleeping man opened his eyes. I flinched back in alarm. He looked round in surprise—just as I had done before earlier, and now he in his own turn seemed to be emerging with difficulty from great depths of confusion. His gaze wandered intently round the strange, unfamiliar room and then fell on me in amazement. But before he spoke, or could quite pull himself together, I had control of myself. I did not let him say a word, I allowed no questions, no confidences; nothing of yesterday or of last night was to be explained, discussed or mulled over again.

'I have to go now,' I told him quickly. 'You stay here and get dressed. I'll meet you at twelve at the entrance to the casino, and I'll take care of everything else.'

And before he could say a word in reply I fled, to be rid of the sight of the room, and without turning back left the hotel whose name I did not know, any more than I knew the name of the stranger with whom I had just spent the night."

Mrs C interrupted her narrative for a moment again, but all the strain and distress had gone from her voice: like a carriage that toils uphill with difficulty but then, having reached the top, rolls swiftly and smoothly down the other side, her account now proceeded more easily:

"Well—so I made haste to my hotel through the morning light of the streets. The drop in the temperature had driven all the hazy mists from the sky above, just as my own distress had been dispelled. For remember what I told you earlier: I had given up my own life entirely after my husband's death. My children did not need me, I didn't care for my own company, and there's no point in a life lived aimlessly. Now, for the first time, a task had suddenly come my way: I had saved a human being, I had exerted all my powers to snatch him back from destruction. There was only a little left to do—for my task must be completed to the end. So I entered my hotel, ignoring the porter's surprise when he saw me returning at nine in the morning—no shame and chagrin over last night's events oppressed me now, I felt my will to live suddenly revive, and an unexpectedly new sense of the point of my existence flowed warmly through my veins. Once in my room I quickly changed my clothes, putting my mourning aside without thinking (as I noticed only later) and choosing a lighter colour instead, went to the bank to withdraw money, and made haste to the station to find out train times. With a determination that surprised me I also made a few other arrangements. Now there was nothing left to do but ensure the departure from Monte Carlo and ultimate salvation of the man whom fate had cast in my way.

It is true that I needed strength to face him personally. Everything yesterday had taken place in the dark, in a vortex; we had been like two stones thrown out of a torrential stream suddenly striking together; we scarcely knew each other face to face, and I wasn't even sure whether the stranger would recognise me again. Yesterday had been chance, frenzy, a case of two confused people possessed; today I must be more open with him, since I must now confront him in the pitiless light of day with myself, my own face, as a living human being.

But it all turned out much easier than I expected. No sooner had I approached the casino at the appointed hour than a young man jumped up from a bench and made haste towards me. There was something so spontaneous, so child-like, unplanned and happy in his surprise and in each of his eloquent movements; he almost flew to me, the radiance of a joy that was both grateful and deferential in his eyes, which were lowered humbly as soon as they felt my confusion in his presence. Gratitude is so seldom found, and those who are most grateful cannot express it, are silent in their confusion, or ashamed, or sometimes seem ungracious just to conceal their feelings. But in this man, the expression of whose every feeling God, like a mysterious sculptor, had made sensual, beautiful, graphic, his gratitude glowed with radiant passion right through his body. He bent over my hand and remained like that for a moment, the narrow line of his boyish head reverently bowed, respectfully brushing kisses on my fingers; only then did he step back, ask how I was, and look at me most movingly. There was such courtesy in everything he said that within a few minutes the last of my anxiety had gone. As if reflecting the lightening of my own feelings, the landscape around was shining, the spell on it broken: the sea that had been disturbed and angry yesterday lay so calm and bright that every pebble beneath the gently breaking surf gleamed white, and the casino, that den of iniquity, looked up with Moorish brightness to the damask sky that was now swept clean. The kiosk with the projecting roof beneath which the pouring rain had forced us to shelter yesterday proved to be a flower stall; great bunches of flowers and foliage lay there in motley confusion, in white, red, other bright colours and green, and a young girl in a colourful blouse was offering them for sale.

I invited him to lunch with me in a small restaurant, and there the young stranger told me the story of his tragic venture. It confirmed my first presentiment when I had seen his trembling, nervously shaking hands on the green table. He came from an old aristocratic family in the Austrian part of Poland, was destined for a diplomatic career, had studied in Vienna and passed his first examination with great success a month ago. As a reward, and to celebrate the occasion, his uncle, a high-ranking general-staff officer, had taken him to the Prater in a cab, and they went to the races. His uncle was lucky with his bets and won three times running; then they ate supper in an elegant restaurant on the strength of the fat wad of banknotes that were the uncle's gains. Next day, again to mark his success in the examinations, the budding diplomat received a sum of money from his father which was as much as his usual monthly allowance. Two days earlier this would have seemed to him a large sum, but now, seeing how easily his uncle had won money, it struck him as trifling and left him indifferent. Directly after dinner, therefore, he went to the races again, laid wild, frenzied bets, and fortune—or rather misfortune—would have it that he left the Prater after the last race with three times the sum he had brought there. Now a mania for gambling infected him; sometimes he went to the races, sometimes to play in coffee houses and clubs, exhausting his time, his studies, his nerves, and above all his money. He was no longer able to think or to sleep peacefully, and he was quite unable to control himself; one night, coming home from a club where he had lost everything, he found a crumpled banknote forgotten in his waistcoat pocket as he was undressing. There was no holding him; he got dressed again and walked the streets until he found a few people playing dominoes in a coffee house, and sat with them until dawn. On one occasion his married sister came to his aid, paying his debts to moneylenders who were very ready to give credit to the heir of a great and noble name. For a while he was lucky at play again—but then matters went inexorably downhill, and the more he lost, the more urgently did unsecured obligations and fixed-term IOUs require him to find relief by winning. He had long ago pawned his watch and his clothes, and at last a terrible thing happened: he stole two large pearl earrings that she seldom wore from his old aunt's dressing table. He pawned one of the pearls for a large sum, which his gambling quadrupled that evening. But instead of redeeming the pearl he staked all his winnings and lost. At the time when he left Vienna the theft had not yet been discovered, so he pawned the second pearl and on a sudden impulse travelled by train to Monte Carlo to win the fortune he dreamt of at roulette. On arrival he had sold his suitcase, his clothes, his umbrella; he had nothing left but a revolver with four cartridges, and a small cross set with jewels given him by his godmother, Princess X. He did not want to part with the cross, but it too had been sold for fifty francs that afternoon, just to let him try to satisfy his urge by playing for life or death one last time that evening.

He told me all this with the captivating charm of his original and lively nature. And I listened shaken, gripped and much moved, but not for a moment did it occur to me to feel horror that the man at my table was in sober fact a thief. Yesterday, if someone had so much as suggested to me that I, a woman with a blameless past who expected the company she kept to be strictly and conventionally virtuous, would be sitting here on familiar terms with a perfectly strange young man, not much older than my son, who had stolen a pair of pearl earrings, I would have thought he had taken leave of his senses and such a thing was impossible. But I felt no horror at all as he told his tale, for he spoke so naturally and passionately that it seemed more like the account of a fever or illness than a crime. Moreover, the word 'impossible' had suddenly lost its meaning for a woman who had known such an unexpected, torrential experience as I had the night before. In those ten hours, I had come to know immeasurably more about reality than in my preceding forty respectable years of life.

Yet something else about his confession did alarm me, and that was the feverish glint in his eyes, which made all the nerves of his face twitch galvanically as he talked about his passion for gambling. Even speaking of it aroused him, and his face graphically and with terrible clarity illustrated that tension between pleasure and torment. His hands, those beautiful, nervous, slender-jointed hands, instinctively began to turn into preying, hunting, fleeing animal creatures again, just as they did at the gaming table. As he spoke I saw them suddenly trembling, beginning at the wrists, arching and clenching into fists, then opening up to intertwine their fingers once more. And when he confessed to the theft of the pearl earrings they suddenly performed a swift, leaping, quick, thieving movement—I involuntarily jumped. I could see his fingers pouncing on the jewels and swiftly stowing them away in the hollow of his clenched hand. And with nameless horror, I recognised that the very last drop of this man's blood was poisoned by his addiction.

That was the one thing that so shattered and horrified me about his tale, the pitiful enslavement of a young, light-hearted, naturally carefree man to a mad passion. I considered it my prime duty to persuade my unexpected protégé, in friendly fashion, that he must leave Monte Carlo, where the temptation was most dangerous, without delay; he must return to his family this very day, before anyone noticed that the pearl earrings were gone and his future was ruined for ever. I promised him money for his journey and to redeem the jewellery, though only on condition that he left today and swore to me, on his honour, never to touch a card or play any other game of chance again.

I shall never forget the passion of gratitude, humble at first, then gradually more ardent, with which that lost stranger listened to me, how he positively drank in my words as I promised him help, and then he suddenly reached both hands over the table to take mine in a gesture I can never forget, a gesture of what one might call adoration and sacred promise. There were tears in his bright but slightly confused eyes; his whole body was trembling nervously with happy excitement. I have tried to describe the uniquely expressive quality of his gestures to you several times already, but I cannot depict this one, for it conveyed ecstatic, supernal delight such as a human countenance seldom turns on us, comparable only to that white shade in which, waking from a dream, we think we see the countenance of an angel vanishing.

Why conceal it? I could not withstand that glance. Gratitude is delightful because it is so seldom found, tender feeling does one good, and such exuberance was delightfully new and heart-warming to me, sober, cool woman that I was. And with that crushed, distressed young man, the landscape itself had revived as if by magic after last night's rain. The sea, calm as a millpond, lay shining blue beneath the sky as we came out of the restaurant, and the only white to be seen was the white of seagulls swooping in that other, celestial blue. You know the Riviera landscape. It is always beautiful, but offers its rich colours to the eye in leisurely fashion, flat as a picture postcard, a lethargic sleeping beauty who admits all glances, imperturbable and almost oriental in her ever-opulent willingness. But sometimes, very occasionally, there are days when this beauty rises up, breaks out, cries out loud, you might say, with gaudy, fanatically sparkling colours, triumphantly flinging her flower-like brightness in your face, glowing, burning with sensuality. And the stormy chaos of the night before had turned to such a lively day, the road was washed white, the sky was turquoise, and everywhere bushes ignited like colourful torches among the lush, drenched green foliage. The mountains seemed suddenly lighter and closer in the cooler, sunny air, as if they were crowding towards the gleaming, polished little town out of curiosity. Stepping outside, you sensed at every glance the challenging, cheering aspect of Nature spontaneously drawing your heart to her. 'Let's hire a carriage and drive along the Corniche,' I said.

The young man nodded enthusiastically: he seemed to be really seeing and noticing the landscape for the first time since his arrival. All he had seen so far was the dank casino hall with its sultry, sweaty smell, its crowds of ugly visitors with their twisted features, and a rough, grey, clamorous sea outside. But now the sunny beach lay spread out before us like a huge fan, and the eye leapt with pleasure from one distant point to another. We drove along the beautiful road in a slow carriage (this was before the days of the motor car), past many villas and many fine views; a hundred times, seeing every house, every villa in the green shade of the pine trees, one felt a secret wish to live there, quiet and content, away from the world!

Was I ever happier in my life than in that hour? I don't know. Beside me in the carriage sat the young man who had been a prey to death and disaster yesterday and now, in amazement, stood in the spray of the sparkling white dome of the sun above; years seemed to have dropped away from him. He had become all boy, a handsome, sportive child with a playful yet respectful look in his eyes, and nothing about him delighted me more than his considerate attentiveness. If the carriage was going up a steep climb which the horses found arduous, he jumped nimbly down to push from behind. If I named a flower or pointed to one by the roadside, he hurried to pluck it. He picked up a little toad that was hopping with difficulty along the road, lured out by last night's rain, and carried it carefully over to the green grass, where it would not be crushed as the carriage went by; and from time to time, in great high spirits, he would say the most delightful and amusing things; I believe he found laughter of that kind a safety valve, and without it he would have had to sing or dance or fool around in some way, so happily inebriated was the expression of his sudden exuberance.

As we were driving slowly through a tiny village high up on the road, he suddenly raised his hat politely. I was surprised and asked who he was greeting, since he was a stranger among strangers here. He flushed slightly at my question and explained, almost apologetically, that we had just passed a church, and at home in Poland, as in all strict Catholic countries, it was usual from childhood on to raise your hat outside any church or other place of worship. I was deeply moved by this exquisite respect for religion, and remembering the cross he had mentioned, I asked if he was a devout believer. When he modestly confessed, with a touch of embarrassment, that he hoped to be granted God's grace, an idea suddenly came to me. 'Stop!' I told the driver, and quickly climbed out of the carriage. He followed me in surprise, asking, 'Where are we going?' I said only, 'Come with me.'

In his company I went back to the church, a small country church built of brick. The interior looked chalky, grey and empty; the door stood open, so that a yellow beam of light cut sharply through the dark, where blue shadows surrounded a small altar. Two candles, like veiled eyes, looked out of the warm, incense-scented twilight. We entered, he took off his hat, dipped his hand in the basin of holy water, crossed himself and genuflected. When he was standing again I took his arm. 'Go and find an altar or some image here that is holy to you,' I urged him, 'and swear the oath I will recite to you.' He looked at me in surprise, almost in alarm. But quickly understanding, he went over to a niche, made the sign of the cross and obediently knelt down. 'Say after me,' I said, trembling with excitement myself, 'say after me: I swear… '—'I swear,' he repeated, and I continued, 'that I will never play for money again, whatever the game may be, I swear that I will never again expose my life and my honour to the dangers of that passion.'

He repeated the words, trembling: they lingered loud and clear in the empty interior. Then it was quiet for a moment, so quiet that you could hear the faint rustling of the trees outside as the wind blew through their leaves. Suddenly he threw himself down like a penitent and, in tones of ecstasy such as I had never heard before, poured out a flood of rapid, confused words in Polish. I did not understand what he was saying, but it was obviously an ecstatic prayer, a prayer of gratitude and remorse, for in his stormy confession he kept bowing his head humbly down on the prayer desk, repeating the strange sounds ever more passionately, and uttering the same word more and more violently and with extraordinary ardour. I have never heard prayer like that before or since, in any church in the world. As he prayed his hands clung convulsively to the wooden prayer desk, his whole body shaken by an internal storm that sometimes caught him up and sometimes cast him down again. He saw and felt nothing else: his whole being seemed to exist in another world, in a purgatorial fire of transmutation, or rising to a holier sphere. At last he slowly stood up, made the sign of the cross, and turned with an effort. His knees were trembling, his countenance was pale as the face of a man exhausted. But when he saw me his eyes beamed, a pure, a truly devout smile lit up his ecstatic face; he came closer, bowed low in the Russian manner, took both my hands and touched them reverently with his lips. 'God has sent you to me. I was thanking him.' I did not know what to say, but I could have wished the organ to crash out suddenly above the low pews, for I felt that I had succeeded: I had saved this man for ever.

We emerged from the church into the radiant, flooding light of that May-like day; the world had never before seemed to me more beautiful. Then we drove slowly on in the carriage for another two hours, taking the panoramic road over the hills which offers a new view at every turn. But we spoke no more. After so much emotion, any other words would have seemed an anti-climax. And when by chance my eyes met his, I had to turn them away as if ashamed, so shaken was I by the sight of my own miracle.

We returned to Monte Carlo at about five in the afternoon. I had an appointment with relatives which I could not cancel at this late date. And in fact I secretly wished for a pause in which to recover from feelings that had been too violently aroused. For this was too much happiness. I felt that I must rest from my overheated, ecstatic condition. I had never known anything like it in my life before. So I asked my protégé to come into my hotel with me for a moment, and there in my room I gave him the money for his journey and to redeem the jewellery. We agreed that while I kept my appointment he would go and buy his ticket, and then we would meet at seven in the entrance hall of the station, half-an-hour before the departure of the train taking him home by way of Genoa. When I was about to give him the five banknotes his lips turned curiously pale. 'No… no money… I beg you, not money!' he uttered through his teeth, while his agitated fingers quivered nervously. 'No money… not money… I can't stand the sight of it!' he repeated, as if physically overcome by nausea or fear. But I soothed him, saying it was only a loan, and if he felt troubled by it then he could give me a receipt. 'Yes, yes… a receipt,' he murmured, looking away, cramming the crumpled notes into his pocket without looking at them, like something sticky that soiled his fingers, and he scribbled a couple of words on a piece of paper in swift, flying characters. When he looked up damp sweat was standing out on his brow; something within seemed to be choking him, and no sooner had he given me the note than an impulse seemed to pass through him and suddenly—I was so startled that I instinctively flinched back—suddenly he fell on his knees and kissed the hem of my dress. It was an indescribable gesture; its overwhelming violence made me tremble all over. A strange shuddering came over me; I was confused, and could only stammer, 'Thank you for showing your gratitude—but do please go now! We'll say goodbye at seven in the station hall.'

He looked at me with a gleam of emotion moistening his eye; for a moment I thought he was going to say something, for a moment it seemed as if he were coming towards me. But then he suddenly bowed deeply again, very deeply, and left the room."

Once again Mrs C interrupted her story. She had risen and gone to the window to look out, and she stood there motionless for a long time. Watching the silhouette of her back, I saw it shiver slightly, and she swayed. All at once she turned back to me with determination, and her hands, until now calm and at rest, suddenly made a violent, tearing movement as if to rip something apart. Then she looked at me with a hard, almost defiant glance, and abruptly began again.

"I promised to be completely honest with you, and now I see how necessary that promise was. For only now that, for the first time, I make myself describe the whole course of those hours exactly as they happened, seeking words for what was a very complicated, confused feeling, only now do I clearly understand much that I did not know at the time, or perhaps would not acknowledge. So I will be firm and will not spare myself, and I will tell you the truth too: then, at the moment when the young man left the room and I remained there alone, I felt—it was a dazed sensation, like swooning—I felt a hard blow strike my heart. Something had hurt me mortally, but I did not know, or refused to know, what, after all, it was in my protégé's touchingly respectful conduct that wounded me so painfully.

But now that I force myself to bring up all the past unsparingly, in proper order, as if it were strange to me, and your presence as a witness allows no pretence, no craven concealment of a feeling which shames me, I clearly see that what hurt so much at the time was disappointment… my disappointment that… that the young man had gone away so obediently… that he did not try to detain me, to stay with me. It was because he humbly and respectfully fell in with my first attempt to persuade him to leave, instead... instead of trying to take me in his arms. It was because he merely revered me as a saint who had appeared to him along his way and did not... did not feel for me as a woman.

That was the disappointment I felt, a disappointment I did not admit to myself either then or later, but a woman's feelings know everything without words, without conscious awareness. For—and now I will deceive myself no longer—for if he had embraced me then, if he had asked me then, I would have gone to the ends of the earth with him, I would have dishonoured my name and the name of my children—I would have eloped with him, caring nothing for what people would say or the dictates of my own reason, just as Madame Henriette ran off with the young Frenchman whom she hadn't even met the day before. I wouldn't have asked where we were going, or how long it would last, I wouldn't have turned to look back at my previous life—I would have sacrificed my money, my name, my fortune and my honour to him, I would have begged in the street for him, there is probably no base conduct in the world to which he could not have brought me. I would have thrown away all that we call modesty and reason if he had only spoken one word, taken one step towards me, if he had tried to touch me—so lost in him was I at that moment. But... as I told you... the young man, in his strangely dazed condition, did not spare another glance for me and the woman in me… and I knew how much, how fervently I longed for him only when I was alone again, when the passion that had just been lighting up his radiant, his positively seraphic face was cast darkly back on me and now lingered in the void of an abandoned breast. With difficulty, I pulled myself together. My appointment was a doubly unwelcome burden. I felt as if a heavy iron helmet were weighing down on my brow and I was swaying under its weight; my thoughts were as disjointed as my footsteps as I at last went over to the other hotel to see my relatives. I sat there in a daze, amidst lively chatter, and was startled whenever I happened to look up and see their unmoved faces, which seemed to me frozen like masks by comparison with that face of his, enlivened as if by the play of light and shade as clouds cross the sky. I found the cheerful company as dreadfully inert as if I were among the dead, and while I put sugar in my cup and joined absently in the conversation, that one face kept coming before my mind's eye, as if summoned up by the surging of the blood. It had become a fervent joy to me to watch that face, and—terrible thought!—in an hour or so I would have seen it for the last time. I must involuntarily have sighed or groaned gently, for my husband's cousin leant over to me: what was the matter, she asked, didn't I feel well? I looked so pale and sad. This unexpected question gave me a quick, easy excuse; I said I did indeed have a migraine, and perhaps she would allow me to slip away.

Thus restored to my own company, I hurried straight to my hotel. No sooner was I alone there than the sense of emptiness and abandonment came over me again, feverishly combined with a longing for the young man I was to leave today for ever. I paced up and down the room, opened shutters for no good reason, changed my dress and my ribbon, suddenly found myself in front of the looking glass again, wondering whether, thus adorned, I might not be able to attract him after all. And I abruptly understood myself: I would do anything not to lose him! Within the space of a violent moment, my wish turned to determination. I ran down to the porter and told him I was leaving today by the night train. Now I had to hurry: I rang for the maid to help me pack—time was pressing—and as we stowed dresses and small items into my suitcases I dreamt of the coming surprise: I would accompany him to the train, and then, at the very last moment, when he was giving me his hand in farewell, I would suddenly get into the carriage with my astonished companion, I would spend that night with him, and the next night—as long as he wanted me. A kind of enchanted, wild frenzy whirled through my blood, sometimes, to the maid's surprise, I unexpectedly laughed aloud as I flung clothes into the suitcases. My senses, I felt from time to time, were all in disorder. And when the man came to take the cases down I stared at him strangely at first: it was too difficult to think of ordinary matters while I was in the grip of such inner excitement.

Time was short; it must be nearly seven, leaving me at most twenty minutes before the train left—but of course, I consoled myself, my arrival would not be a farewell now, since I had decided to accompany him on his journey as long and as far as he would have me. The hotel manservant carried the cases on ahead while I made haste to the reception desk to settle my bill. The manager was already giving me change, I was about to go on my way, when a hand gently touched my shoulder. I gave a start. It was my cousin; concerned by my apparent illness, she had come to see how I was. Everything went dark before my eyes. I did not want her here; every second I was detained meant disastrous delay, yet courtesy obliged me at least to fall into conversation with her briefly. 'You must go to bed,' she was urging me. 'I'm sure you have a temperature.' And she could well have been right, for the blood was pounding at my temples, and sometimes I felt the blue haze of approaching faintness come over my eyes. But I fended off her suggestions and took pains to seem grateful, while every word burned me, and I would have liked to thrust her ill-timed concern roughly away. However, she stayed and stayed and stayed with her unwanted solicitude, offered me eau de Cologne, would not be dissuaded from dabbing the cool perfume on my temples herself. Meanwhile I was counting the minutes, thinking both of him and of how to find an excuse to escape the torment of her sympathy. And the more restless I became, the more alarming did my condition seem to her; finally she was trying, almost by force, to make me go to my room and lie down. Then—in the middle of her urging—I suddenly saw the clock in the hotel lobby: it was two minutes before seven-thirty, and the train left at seven thirty-five. Brusquely, abruptly, with the brutal indifference of a desperate woman I simply stuck my hand out to my cousin—'Goodbye, I must go!'—and without a moment's thought for her frozen glance, without looking round, I rushed past the surprised hotel staff and out of the door, into the street and down it to the station. From the agitated gesticulating of the hotel manservant standing waiting there with my luggage I saw, well before I got there, that time must be very short. Frantically I ran to the barrier, but there the conductor turned me back—I had forgotten to buy a ticket. And as I almost forcibly tried to persuade him to let me on the platform all the same, the train began to move. I stared at it, trembling all over, hoping at least to catch a glimpse of him at the window of one of the carriages, a wave, a greeting. But in the middle of the hurrying throng I could not see his face. The carriages rolled past faster and faster, and after a minute nothing was left before my darkened eyes but black clouds of steam.

I must have stood there as if turned to stone, for God knows how long; the hotel servant had probably spoken to me in vain several times before he ventured to touch my arm. Only then did I start and come to myself. Should he take my luggage back to the hotel, he asked. It took me a few minutes to think; no, that was impossible, after this ridiculous, frantic departure I couldn't go back there, and I never wanted to again; so I told him, impatient to be alone, to take my cases to the left luggage office. Only then, in the middle of the constantly renewed crush of people flowing clamorously into the hall and then ebbing away again, did I try to think, to think clearly, to save myself from my desperate, painful, choking sense of fury, remorse and despair, for—why not admit it?—the idea that I had missed our last meeting through my own fault was like a knife turning pitilessly within me, burning and sharp. I could have screamed aloud: that red-hot blade, penetrating ever more mercilessly, hurt so much. Perhaps only those who are strangers to passion know such sudden outbursts of emotion in their few passionate moments, moments of emotion like an avalanche or a hurricane; whole years fall from one's own breast with the fury of powers left unused. Never before or after have I felt anything like the astonishment and raging impotence of that moment when, prepared to take the boldest of steps—prepared to throw away my whole carefully conserved, collected, controlled life all at once—I suddenly found myself facing a wall of senselessness against which my passion could only beat its head helplessly.

As for what I did then, how could it be anything but equally senseless? It was foolish, even stupid, and I am almost ashamed to tell you—but I have promised myself and you to keep nothing back. I… well, I went in search of him again. That is to say, I went in search of every moment I had spent with him. I felt irresistibly drawn to everywhere we had been together the day before, the bench in the casino grounds from which I had made him rise, the gaming hall where I had first seen him—yes, even that den of vice, just to relive the past once more, only once more. And tomorrow I would go along the Corniche in a carriage, retracing our path, so that every word and gesture would revive in my mind again—so senseless and childish was my state of confusion. But you must take into account the lightning speed with which these events overwhelmed me—I had felt little more than a single numbing blow, but now, woken too abruptly from that tumult of feeling, I wanted to go back over what I had so fleetingly experienced step by step, relishing it in retrospect by virtue of that magical self-deception we call memory. Well, some things we either do or do not understand. Perhaps you need a burning heart to comprehend them fully.

So I went first to the gaming hall to seek out the table where he had been sitting, and think of his hands among all the others there. I went in: I remembered that I had first seen him at the left-hand table in the second room. Every one of his movements was still clear before my mind's eye: I could have found his place sleepwalking, with my eyes closed and my hands outstretched. So I went in and crossed the hall. And then… as I looked at the crowd from the doorway… then something strange happened. There, in the very place where I dreamt of him, there sat—ah, the hallucinations of fever!—there sat the man himself. He looked exactly as I had seen him in my daydream just now—exactly as he had been yesterday, his eyes fixed on the ball, pale as a ghost—but he it unmistakably was.

I was so shocked that I felt as if I must cry out. But I controlled my alarm at this ridiculous vision and closed my eyes. 'You're mad—dreaming feverish,' I told myself. 'It's impossible. You're hallucinating. He left half-an-hour ago.' Only then did I open my eyes again. But terrible to relate, he was still sitting there exactly as he had been sitting just now, in the flesh and unmistakable. I would have known those hands among millions… no, I wasn't dreaming, he was real. He had not left as he had promised he would, the madman was sitting there, he had taken the money I gave him for his journey and brought it here, to the green table, gambling it on his passion, oblivious of all else, while I was desperately eating my heart out for him.

I abruptly moved forwards: fury blurred my vision, a frenzied, red-eyed, raging desire to take the perjurer who had so shamefully abused my confidence, my feelings, my devotion by the throat. But I controlled myself. With a deliberately slow step (and how much strength that cost me!) I went up to the table to sit directly opposite him. A gentleman courteously made way for me. Two metres of green cloth stood between us, and as if looking down from a balcony at a play on stage I could watch his face, the same face that I had seen two hours ago radiant with gratitude, illuminated by the aura of divine grace, and now entirely absorbed in the infernal fires of his passion again. The hands, those same hands that I had seen clinging to the wood of the prayer desk as he swore a most sacred oath, were now clutching at the money again like the claws of lustful vampires. For he had been winning, he must have won a very great deal: in front of him shone a jumbled pile of jettons and louis d'ors and banknotes, a disordered medley in which his quivering, nervous fingers were stretching and bathing with delight. I saw them pick up separate notes, stroke and fold them, I saw them turn and caress coins, then suddenly and abruptly catch up a fistful and put them down on one of the spaces. And immediately that spasmodic tic around his nostrils began again, the call of the croupier tore his greedily blazing eyes away from the money to the spinning ball, he seemed to be flowing out of himself, as it were, while his elbows might have been nailed to the green table. His total addiction was revealed as even more dreadful, more terrible than the evening before, for every move he made murdered that other image within me, the image shining as if on a golden ground that I had credulously swallowed.

So we sat there two metres away from each other; I was staring at him, but he was unaware of me. He was not looking at me or anyone else, his glance merely moved to the money, flickering unsteadily with the ball as it rolled back to rest: all his senses were contained, chasing back and forth, in that one racing green circle. To this obsessive gambler the whole world, the whole human race had shrunk to a rectangular patch of cloth. And I knew that I could stand here for hours and hours, and he would not have the faintest idea of my presence.

But I could stand it no longer. Coming to a sudden decision, I walked round the table, stepped behind him and firmly grasped his shoulder with my hand. His gaze swung upwards, for a second he stared strangely at me, glassy-eyed, like a drunk being laboriously shaken awake, eyes still vague and drowsy, clouded by inner fumes. Then he seemed to recognise me, his mouth opened, quivering, he looked happily up at me and stammered quietly, in a confused tone of mysterious confidentiality, 'It's going well… I knew it would as soon as I came in and saw that he was here… ' I did not understand what he meant. All I saw was that this madman was intoxicated by the game and had forgotten everything else, his promise, his appointment at the station, me and the whole world besides. But even when he was in this obsessive mood I found his ecstasy so captivating that instinctively I went along with him and asked, taken aback, who was here?

'Over there, the one-armed old Russian general,' he whispered, pressing close to me so that no one else would overhear the magic secret. 'Over there, with the white sideboards and the servant behind him. He always wins, I was watching him yesterday, he must have a system, and I always pick the same number... He was winning yesterday too, but I made the mistake of playing on when he had left... that was my error... he must have won twenty thousand francs yesterday, he's winning every time now too, and I just keep following his lead. Now—'

He broke off in mid-sentence, for the hoarse-voiced croupier was calling his '*Faites votre jeu!*' and his glance was already moving away, looking greedily at the place where the white-whiskered Russian sat, nonchalant and grave, thoughtfully putting first one gold coin and then, hesitantly, another on the fourth space. Immediately the fevered hands before me dug into the pile of money and put down a handful of coins on the same place. And when, after a minute, the croupier cried '*Zéro!*' and his rake swept the whole table bare with a single movement, he stared at the money streaming away as if at some marvel. But do you think he turned to me? No he had forgotten all about me; I had dropped out of his life, I was lost and gone from it, his whole being was intent only on the Russian general who, with complete indifference, was hefting two more gold coins in his hand, not yet sure what number to put them on.

I cannot describe my bitterness and despair. But think of my feelings: to be no more than a fly brushed carelessly aside by a man to whom one has offered one's whole life. Once again that surge of fury came over me. I seized his arm with all my strength. He started.

'You will get up at once!' I whispered to him in a soft but commanding tone. 'Remember what you swore in church today, you miserable perjurer.'

He stared at me, perplexed and pale. His eyes suddenly took on the expression of a beaten dog, his lips quivered. All at once he seemed to be remembering the past, and a horror of himself appeared to come over him.

'Yes, yes… ' he stammered. 'Oh, my God, my God… yes, I'm coming, oh, forgive me… '

And his hand was already sweeping the money together, fast at first, gathering it all up with a vehement gesture, but then gradually slowing down, as if coming up against some opposing force. His eyes had fallen once more on the Russian general, who had just made his bet.

'Just a moment,' he said, quickly throwing five gold coins on the same square. 'Just this one more time… I promise you I'll come then—just this one more game… just… '

And again his voice fell silent. The ball had begun to roll and was carrying him away with it. Once again the addict had slipped away from me, from himself, flung round with the tiny ball circling in the smooth hollow of the wheel where it leapt and sprang. Once again the croupier called out the number, once again the rake carried his five coins away from him; he had lost. But he did not turn round. He had forgotten me, just like his oath in the church and the promise he had given me a minute ago. His greedy hand was moving spasmodically towards the dwindling pile of money again, and his intoxicated gaze moved only to the magnet of his will, the man opposite who brought good luck.

My patience was at an end. I shook him again, hard this time. 'Get up at once! Immediately! You said one more game… '

But then something unexpected happened. He suddenly swung round, but the face looking at me was no longer that of a humbled and confused man, it was the face of a man in a frenzy, all anger, with burning eyes and furiously trembling lips. 'Leave me alone!' he spat. 'Go away! You bring me bad luck. Whenever you're here I lose. You brought bad luck yesterday and you're bringing bad luck now. Go away!'

I momentarily froze, but now my own anger was whipped up beyond restraint by his folly.

'I am bringing you bad luck?' I snapped at him. 'You liar, you thief—you promised me… ' But I got no further, for the maniac leapt up from his seat and, indifferent to the turmoil around him, thrust me away. 'Leave me alone,' he cried, losing all control. 'I'm not under your control… here, take your money.' And he threw me a few hundred-franc notes. 'Now leave me alone!'

He had been shouting out loud like a madman, ignoring the hundred or so people around us. They were all staring, whispering, pointing, laughing—other curious onlookers even crowded in from the hall next door. I felt as if my clothes were being torn from my body, leaving me naked before all these prying eyes. '*Silence, madame, s'il vous plaît,*' said the croupier in commanding tones, tapping his rake on the table. He meant me, the wretched creature meant me. Humiliated, overcome by shame, I stood there before the hissing, whispering curious folk like a prostitute whose customer has just thrown money at her. Two hundred, three hundred shameless eyes were turned on my face, and then—then, as I turned my gaze evasively aside, overwhelmed by this filthy deluge of humiliation and shame, my own eyes met two others, piercing and astonished—it was my cousin looking at me appalled, her mouth open, one hand raised as if in horror.

That struck home; before she could stir or recover from her surprise I stormed out of the hall. I got as far as the bench outside, the same bench on which the gambling addict had collapsed yesterday. I dropped to the hard, pitiless wood, as powerless, exhausted and shattered as he had been.

All that is twenty-four years ago, yet when I remember the moment when I stood there before a thousand strangers, lashed by their scorn, the blood freezes in my veins. And once again I feel, in horror, how weak, poor and flabby a substance whatever we call by the names of soul, spirit or feeling must be after all, not to mention what we describe as pain, since all this, even to the utmost degree, is insufficient to destroy the suffering flesh of the tormented body entirely—for we do survive such hours and our blood continues to pulse, instead of dying and falling like a tree struck by lightning. Only for a sudden moment, for an instant, did this pain tear through my joints so hard that I dropped on the bench breathless and dazed, with a positively voluptuous premonition that I must die. But as I was saying, pain is cowardly, it gives way before the overpowering will to live which seems to cling more strongly to our flesh than all the mortal suffering of the spirit. Even to myself, I cannot explain my feelings after such a shattering blow, but I did rise to my feet, although I did not know what to do. Suddenly it occurred to me that my suitcases were already at the station, and I thought suddenly that I must get away, away from here, away from this accursed, this infernal building. Taking no notice of anyone, I made haste to the station and asked when the next train for Paris left. At ten o'clock, the porter told me, and I immediately retrieved my luggage. Ten o'clock—so exactly twenty-four hours had passed since that terrible meeting, twenty-four hours so full of changeable, contradictory feelings that my inner world was shattered for ever. At first, however, I felt nothing but that one word in the constantly hammering, pounding rhythm: away, away, away! The pulses behind my brow kept driving it into my temples like a wedge: away, away, away! Away from this town, away from myself, home to my own people, to my own old life! I travelled through the night to Paris, changed from one station to another and travelled direct to Boulogne, from Boulogne to Dover, from Dover to London, from London to my son's house—all in one headlong flight, without stopping to think or consider, forty-eight hours without sleep, without speaking to anyone, without eating, forty-eight hours during which the wheels of all the trains rattled out that one word: away, away, away! When at last I arrived unexpectedly at my son's country house, everyone was alarmed; there must have been something in my bearing and my eyes that gave me away. My son came to embrace and kiss me, but I shrank away: I could not bear the thought of his touching lips that I felt were disgraced. I avoided all questions, asked only for a bath, because I needed to wash not only the dirt of the journey from my body but all of the passion of that obsessed, unworthy man that seemed to cling to it. Then I dragged myself up to my room and slept a benumbed and stony sleep for twelve or fourteen hours, a sleep such as I have never slept before or since, and after it I know what it must be like to lie dead in a coffin. My family cared for me as for a sick woman, but their affection only hurt me, I was ashamed of their respect, and had to keep preventing myself from suddenly screaming out loud how I had betrayed, forgotten and abandoned them all for the sake of a foolish, crazy passion.

Then, aimless again, I went back to France and a little town where I knew no one, for I was pursued by the delusion that at the very first glance everyone could see my shame and my changed nature from the outside, I felt so betrayed, so soiled to the depths of my soul. Sometimes, when I woke in my bed in the morning, I felt a dreadful fear of opening my eyes. Once again I would be overcome by the memory of that night when I suddenly woke beside a half-naked stranger, and then, as I had before, all I wanted was to die immediately.

But after all, time is strong, and age has the curious power of devaluing all our feelings. You feel death coming closer, its shadow falls black across your path, and things seem less brightly coloured, they do not go to the heart so much, they lose much of their dangerous violence. Gradually I recovered from the shock, and when, many years later, I met a young Pole who was an attaché of the Austrian Embassy at a party, and in answer to my enquiry about that family he told me that one of his cousin's sons had shot himself ten years before in Monte Carlo, I did not even tremble. It hardly hurt any more; perhaps—why deny one's egotism?—I was even glad of it, for now my last fear of ever meeting him again was gone. I had no witness against me left but my own memory. Since then I have become calmer. Growing old, after all, means that one no longer fears the past.

And now you will understand why I suddenly brought myself to tell you about my own experience. When you defended Madame Henriette and said, so passionately, that twenty-four hours could determine a woman's whole life, I felt that you meant me; I was grateful to you, since for the first time I felt myself, as it were, confirmed in my existence. And then I thought it would be good to unburden myself of it all for once, and perhaps then the spell on me would be broken, the eternal looking back; perhaps I can go to Monte Carlo tomorrow and enter the same hall where I met my fate without feeling hatred for him or myself. Then the stone will roll off my soul, laying its full weight over the past and preventing it from ever rising again. It has done me good to tell you all this. I feel easier in my mind now and almost light at heart… thank you for that."

With these words she had suddenly risen, and I felt that she had reached the end. Rather awkwardly, I sought for something to say. But she must have felt my emotion, and quickly waved it away.

"No, please, don't speak… I'd rather you didn't reply or say anything to me. Accept my thanks for listening, and I wish you a good journey."

She stood opposite me, holding out her hand in farewell. Instinctively I looked at her face, and the countenance of this old woman who stood before me with a kindly yet slightly ashamed expression seemed to me wonderfully touching. Whether it was the reflection of past passion or mere confusion that suddenly dyed her cheeks with red, the colour rising to her white hair, she stood there just like a girl, in a bridal confusion of memories and ashamed of her own confession. Involuntarily moved, I very much wanted to say something to express my respect for her, but my throat was too constricted. So I leant down and respectfully kissed the faded hand that trembled slightly like an autumn leaf.

MORE FROM

STEFAN ZWEIG

TWO COLLECTIONS OF
HIS MOST SCINTILLATING
SHORT STORIES

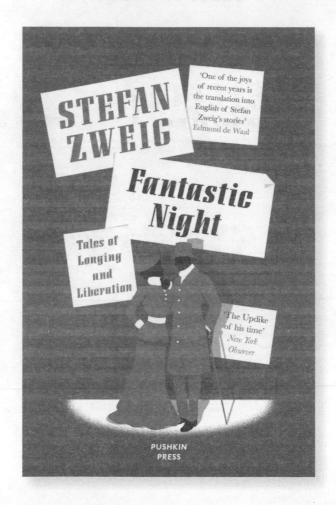

STEFAN ZWEIG

The Invisible Collection

Tales of Obsession and Desire

PUSHKIN PRESS

HIS ONLY FINISHED NOVEL –
TENSE, POWERFUL,
DEVASTATINGLY ACUTE.

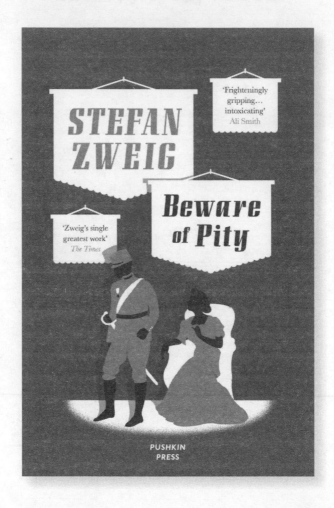